Amelia's

7th-Grade Notebook

by Marissa Moss

(except all 7th-grade experiences
verifiably Amelia's!)

Simon & Schuster Books for Young Readers

New York   London   Toronto   Sydney

JUL   2012   CH

This notebook is dedicated to
Mollie Katzen,

who is beautiful without a drop
of makeup!

SIMON & SCHUSTER BOOKS FOR YOUNG READERS
An imprint of Simon & Schuster Children's Publishing Division
1230 Avenue of the Americas, New York, New York 10020
Copyright © 2007 by Marissa Moss

Another
beautiful → A Paula Wiseman Book
woman!

SIMON & SCHUSTER BOOKS FOR YOUNG READERS
is a trademark of Simon & Schuster, Inc.

Amelia ® and the notebook design are
registered trademarks of Marissa Moss.

Book design by Amelia   Thanks,
(with help from Lucy Ruth Cummins)   Lucy!

The text for this book is hand-lettered.
Manufactured in China

2 4 6 8 10 9 7 5 3 1

CIP data for this book is available from the Library
of Congress.

ISBN-13: 978-1-4169-3661-9   ISBN-10: 1-4169-3661-0

* first *
edition

Amelia's 7th-Grade Notebook

So this is _this_ is what a 7th grader looks like!

7th Grade!

I can hardly believe I'm in 7th grade now! I mean, that's practically high school, where my sister, Cleo, is this year. That's one great thing about starting 7th grade — since Cleo's starting 9th grade, she's not in the same school as me anymore.

HOOORAY!!!

No more seeing Cleo in the halls or cafeteria or library or ANYWHERE! I'm free, FREE, FREE!

Another reason 7th grade is so much better than 6th is that now I'm an expert at using a locker and switching classes every period. Last year, everything was strange and new and scary. This year it'll be easy.

The last big reason 7th grade is great is that I only have the evil Mr. Lambaste for study hall (which doesn't really count

So far I like my classes and the best part is that Carly is in 3 of them — social studies, English, and French. Too bad we don't have science and P.E. together like we did last year, but I'm not complaining — I get to be with my best friend and I have all new, nice teachers. None of them have Mr. Lambaste's mean unibrow and scowl.

One look from him could sour the whole day.

A glare from him ruined the whole week.

And if he actually said something — his usual ugly insults — that was it for the month.

I had him for 2 classes last year — English and social studies — doubling the misery.

Now for English, I have Ms. Hanover. She actually likes students — a big change from Mr. L.!

For social studies, I have Mr. Yegg. (We call him "Egg.") He's so young, he almost looks like a student himself. (If he shaved, he definitely would!) He's the most energetic teacher I've ever seen. I almost expect him to do calisthenics in front of the class, he's so charged up!

Instead, he has a basketball hoop. If you answer a question right, you get to try for a basket. If you score, you win candy. That's my kind of teacher!

The rest of my teachers are good too. The only one who might be a problem is Ms. Castor, the P.E. teacher. She takes her class very seriously, which is bad news for me since P.E. is the subject I take the least seriously. I mean, it's not educational or interesting. It's just to keep us in shape (which I can do on my own, thanks). I don't mind exercise. I know it's important. It's the competitive edge I hate — that and the fact I'm terrible at every sport known to man. Since I'm good at drawing, you'd think I would have good hand-eye coordination. I don't.

But even playing volleyball (which naturally I'm horrible at) couldn't ruin today. The principal announced the first dance of the year and it's only for 7th graders — my first chance to do a truly 7th-grade thing! Too bad it's a dance thing. I'm a little excited about going and a lot nervous.

I've never been to a dance, but I know there's loud music and you're supposed to gyrate wildly — that's the dancing part. Luckily, there's no wrong way to dance — you just move to the music and hope you have some sense of rhythm.

At lunch everyone was talking about the dance. Even the walls were suddenly covered with posters blaring at us to COME TO THE DANCE!

The more Carly and Leah chattered, the less I felt like going. The dance was beginning to sound like the kind of thing I'm terrible at. Even worse than volleyball.

And there was no escape — the dance was EVERYWHERE!

dance steps or missteps?   Can you fail at dancing after all?

I could just imagine it — Carly and Leah happily dancing away in their cool clothes while I stood there, miserable, looking like a complete dork. It'll be a nightmare! Now I'm not sure if I want to go at all, but I don't know how to explain that to Carly. Those kinds of things are so easy for her.

Walking home from school, I tried to hint that I might not go to the dance after all. I used the first excuse that popped into my head. Usually it's better to think of these things beforehand, but there wasn't time.

Um, you know, Carly, about the dance...

...I think it's the same night I promised Mom I'd shampoo the rugs. If I don't, I'll lose my allowance.

Shampoo the rugs? Are you kidding? Who does that kind of thing in the evening?

And since when have you washed the carpets in your house?

Since never, which is why we need to do it now.

I'm sure your mom can wait until the weekend like a normal person.

"No, she can't because there's a special bargain price for Friday nights. Like you said, no one washes rugs then, so they're trying to encourage customers."

"Does it have to be that Friday night? Why not the next one?"

The bad thing about lying is that you have to invent more and more lies to cover the original lie, and each new lie has to be convincing or the whole elaborate series of lies topples. →

It was like building a house of cards, holding my breath in case the next lie would be the one to make the whole delicate construction collapse. ↓

"Because, um, because, oh, I remember — because the next Friday, Mom has her book group, so that won't work."

"You know how Cleo is..."

"And Cleo can't help? It has to be you?"

"Yeah, and I know how YOU are, and you're making the whole thing up! Why? Don't you want to go?"

It was too exhausting to lie any more. Plus I wasn't good at it. The house of cards was about to tumble. So I told Carly the truth. I said I was afraid that no one would ask me to dance and I'd be labeled a loser for the rest of my life — or at least the rest of the year. I wanted to feel good about 7th grade, not depressed.

"Come on," Carly urged. "It'll be fun. I promise. We'll go together."

Easy for her to say. Someone would ask her to dance, for sure. She'd have fun, not me. I hated that it mattered so much to me, but it did. What happened at the first dance in 7th grade would seal my reputation in cement. In 6th grade you're still a little kid because you're the youngest group in middle school, so stuff doesn't matter as much. But 7th grade is something else entirely.

"Amelia! It's a dance, not a death sentence. You're way too serious!"

Carly wasn't going to give up, and maybe she was right. It was one small dance, right? Not something that would make or break my reputation in middle school.

← So I said yes.

All right, I'll go. But you have to promise NOT to abandon me. PROMISE?

Carly grinned. "Promise!"

Okay, I gave in, I said yes, but maybe I'll conveniently get food poisoning on Friday. Or the flu. Or even amnesia. I might have to break into my secret stash of emergency excuses.

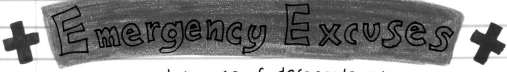

Emergency Excuses

To be used in case of desperate crises — when you really, REALLY don't want to go somewhere and you need an OUT!

Highly Contagious
Ickiness
↓

Family Duty that
No One Else Would Do
↓

I'd go, but I have lice and I have to wash EVERYTHING — me, my clothes, the furniture, the rugs, the walls...

My baby half-brother is visiting and someone has to watch him and change his diapers. Unless you want to.

Burdensome Chore
↓

When Mom says it's time to clean the oven, I just put on the rubber gloves and do it. There's NO arguing with her about it — NONE!

Conflict of Interest
↓

I _would_ go to the dance, but my archenemy will be there and if we're ever in the same room at the same time, the world will IMPLODE! You didn't know I _had_ an archenemy? Of course I do! Doesn't everybody?

Time-Sensitive Demand
↓

It was time to turn the compost, so I _had_ to get right to it. You know how sensitive compost is — if you don't turn it at just the right moment, months of work are wasted!

Natural Disaster
↓

I was on my way there when the car fell into a sinkhole. We were trapped for two days!

HELP!

If none of those work, here's the Top-Rated Emergency Excuse. Don't go to whatever it is you're trying to avoid and, the next day, say:

It was horrible! You wouldn't believe it — I was abducted by aliens!

Uh-huh, sure.

No, really — you've GOT to believe me!

Hi, Mom!

Believe her — we're real!

Here's the proof, a note written in Alienese.

It says:
"Please excuse the bearer from any activity. They were abducted and unavailable at the required time. Thank you for your patience."

At dinner, Mom mentioned the dance and that changed things completely. Now I _have_ to go.

↓

Amelia, I see in the parent newsletter that the first 7th grade dance is this Friday. Are you going?

Are you kidding? Amelia? Why bother? She'll just stand around writing in her notebook all night.

I will not! And I AM going. It'll be fun. Carly and I are going to have a GREAT time.

Cleo rolled her eyes. "Just don't come crying to me when nobody asks you to dance."

"Don't be ridiculous," Mom said. "Of course some boy will ask Amelia to dance. She's very pretty."

Pretty? I'm pretty? I never really thought about that. And you have to be pretty for a boy to want to dance with you? Why should the boy have the power of choosing? Why can't I pick a boy _I_ think is cute to dance with me? Why do I have to wait for someone to approve of me? Is this what being in 7th grade means — suddenly having to worry about whether you're pretty or not?

This dance is sounding worse and worse. It's like a brutal initiation into teenagerhood, not a fun party.

I stared at myself in the bathroom mirror for a long time, trying to figure out if I'm pretty or not. I'm still not sure.
↓

hair - nothing special - not bad and not good, either, but better than being bald or a total tangled mess, so that's something.

eyes - I think they're the best part of my face, large and green — what's not to like?

nose - at least it's not a jelly-roll nose, though it's not exactly cute and perky. I guess it's okay.

okay, no earrings — I know that's bad, but Mom won't let me pierce my ears, so what can I do?

mouth and teeth — no major defects here, so pretty good, I think.

chin - what makes a pretty chin? I have no idea!

I'm so used to my face as _me_ that it's hard for me to look at it and judge it like it belongs to a stranger. Am I pretty? I hope so. I'm not ugly, but maybe I'm plain. Plain is definitely not good, but can be improved with makeup. If I wore makeup. Which I don't. But if I'm plain, maybe I should. Except I don't know how and I don't want to. It's all so CONFUSING!

Definitely ugly - yuech!
↓

Plain, _not_ pretty, but not ugly either
↓

Once I started thinking about whether or not I was pretty, I couldn't stop. I tried to remember Dad's face when he first saw me a couple of years ago. Was he disappointed because I was ugly? Was he relieved because I was prettier than the last time he'd seen me as a wrinkly, bald baby? Then when we went to the big family reunion and I first met our cousin Justin, did he think I was pretty? I know he thought Cleo was, because another cousin caught them kissing in the barn. Which is really confusing because I would have said there's no way Cleo's pretty, absolutely none. And that's not just my biased opinion. It's pure fact.

hair - it covers her head - that's it

thick eyebrows that are just a hair too close together

Cleo's best feature is her eyes - big and brown with thick eyelashes - but that's the end of the list of good things.

jelly-roll nose - need I say more?

big, rubbery lips - I guess some people could consider these a plus, but seeing them chomp and chew is enough to turn them into a big minus.

So maybe being pretty isn't so important afterall. Or maybe one person's ugly is another person's pretty. That's the kind of thing Mom would say. I'm not sure I believe it. If you watch TV or movies, you can see that there's a certain standard, a way girls are supposed to look.

EYES

The color doesn't matter — the important thing for beautiful eyes is that they're big (but not bulgy) with thick,  dark eyelashes.

Squinty, narrow eyes or eyes with no lashes are in the yuck category. But if the rest of the face is beautiful and only the eyes aren't pretty, what does that mean for the whole face? How many pretty parts add up to a pretty whole? Does it matter which parts are pretty?

NOSES

There's a lot of room for a variety of noses to fit into the pretty category because a lot depends on the size of the nose in proportion to the face. It's funny that big eyes are best, but big noses are _not_. So long as the nose isn't too big or bumpy or potato-y or odd-shaped, it's fine.

Bad eyes don't cancel out the rest of a pretty face, but a bad nose does. No matter how beautiful the other parts are, if the nose is huge and hulking, that's all you'll see.

It's sad but true. A bad nose ← can cancel out everything else.

But then Cleo comes along and proves the opposite. She has a HUGE nose, but boys still like her. Is she pretty? Or is she something else, so her looks don't matter? →

MOUTHS AND TEETH

↑ Pointy lips   ↑ pouty lips   ↑ long lips   ↑ curvy lips   ↑ wide lips   ↑ no lips

All lips seem good to me except no lips at all. I don't think the shape matters as much as the expression they have. Smiling is definitely prettier than frowning.

For teeth, the main thing is if they're crooked or not. Braces are okay — they're like jewelry for the mouth. And it matters if the teeth are CLEAN. Green teeth are NEVER pretty!

↑ good teeth   ↑ crooked teeth— waiting for braces   ↑ fuzzy, green teeth — GROSS!   ↑ blinding white teeth— wow!

After thinking about the possibilities, I decided my face isn't bad at all. At least I don't look ANYTHING like Cleo! I'm not sure if I'm pretty or not, but my face is definitely expressive. And it feels like me. It would be awful to have a face that didn't match how you saw yourself.

At school the next day I asked Carly if she thinks I'm pretty. She said of course I am. But maybe she just said that because we're friends. There's no good way to tell a friend she's ugly. Still, if I really _am_ ugly, she'd have avoided the whole topic, the way you do when you don't want to tell someone the truth but you don't want to lie either.

HOW NOT TO LIE, BUT NOT TELL THE TRUTH

change the subject ↓

say bland generalities that mean nothing ↓

pretend you didn't hear the question ↙

Look, over there! Is that Superman?

A friend in need is a friend indeed, don't you agree?

Some people say beauty is in the eye of the beholder. I say, whatever!

La la la la la la la!

It's a strange coincidence that I'm thinking about what I look like so much because in art Ms. Oates (who wants us to call her "Star," but I just CAN'T) is having us do self-portraits.

Now, class, I want each of you to come up with an image that represents the real you.

It can be a realistic portrayal of your face or something else entirely. Students have been very creative with this.

One student made a collage with family photos.

Another student cut words out of magazines and assembled them into an image of his face.

And another, who was exploring her Japanese heritage, did a cut-paper piece using origami.

"You can see," said Ms. Oates, "the possibilities are as different as each of you. I expect to see some distinctive work, pieces bursting with personality."

Leah winked at me and whispered, "Some personalities are better kept under wraps. Think of Maxine's — she'd have to add stink to whatever she made to capture the real flavor of who she is."

Leah is in the same art class as me. She's a good artist.

Yeah. If she had to pick her own name to match her character, like the way Ms. Oates wants to be "Star," Maxine would have to be "Nasty."

I think I'm a pretty good artist too.

It's true that Maxine is mean, but I'm sure she doesn't see herself that way. She'd probably call herself "Glamour" or draw herself as a supermodel even though she's master of the Ugly Anonymous Note. Which made me wonder — how clearly do we see ourselves? I might think I'm pretty when really I'm not.

I may not be able to judge whether my face is pretty or not, but one thing I know for sure...

... it fits me. Just like my name fits me. I wouldn't want another name. I couldn't imagine being called "Eugenia" or "Harriet." And I like that my dad picked "Amelia." It gives me some connection to him.

I was thinking about names, but Leah was thinking about the dance.

"Aren't you excited about it?" she asked. "We're 7th graders now — we need to celebrate! We're not the bottom of the heap anymore. We're experienced survivors of one year of middle school. It's great we get a dance so early in the year to congratulate us."

I guess that's one way to look at it. I agree that 7th grade is better than 6th because at least we're used to middle school. But I'm not used to dances.

I watched the 6th graders panicking as they tried to open their lockers and I was so glad that wasn't me anymore. The new 6th graders look so young and they're always getting lost — like I did.

The first week in 7th grade went pretty well. I like my teachers. I get to have Carly and Leah in some of my classes, and Maxine is in _none_ of them. Plus Cleo's not even in the same school anymore. It's the perfect start to a perfect year. Except tonight's the dance and that might ruin everything! After only a few good days, I'm afraid the whole year will be ruined. I'm _trying_ to be positive — really, I am. Carly promised we'll go together and Leah said she'll meet us there, so there'll be a good beginning. Maybe the rest will be okay too.

That's what I hoped, but Cleo took care of that. She took one look at me and destroyed any illusion I had that I could have fun.

You're wearing THAT? And what did you do to your hair? Why aren't you at least wearing lip gloss? You look so scrawny, if you stood sideways, you'd be a Zipper. You look TERRIBLE!

So much for sweet, sisterly concern!

Thanks a lot, Cleo! I had tried to look pretty, I really had. Carly had lent me something cute to wear, so I know my clothes weren't dorky. But I couldn't borrow Carly's face or her style. No matter how I dressed myself up, I was still me. I didn't know how lip gloss or different hair could change that.

I sat outside on the front steps, waiting for Carly and feeling miserable.

This was fun?

When Carly saw me, she knew just what to do. She sat down next to me, put her arm around me, and gave me a big hug.

"Why are you so sad?" she asked.

I told her about Cleo.

"And you're listening to her?" Carly laughed. "Like she knows anything about looking good!"

I started to laugh too. Carly was right — what did Cleo know? Just because she was older didn't make her an expert on ANYTHING. Why should I care about her opinion? I shouldn't and I won't!

"Come on," Carly said. "You look great, especially when you smile. Now let's go to the dance."

So we did. And next to Carly, I actually felt pretty. But she was more than pretty — she was beautiful.

I've always thought Carly was cute, but tonight was something else.

she was wearing eyeliner and lip gloss, something I've never seen her do before.

← That made her look even more glamorous.

If I wore those things, I'd look like I was trying too hard.

And I still wouldn't look good.

With Carly, it was clear she really was pretty — it wasn't just the make up.

And it wasn't just my opinion. As soon as we walked into the dance, Aldo came up to her and asked her to dance. She whispered to me, "You're next," and then she was gone.

I tried to look happy and perky, the kind of girl a boy would want to dance with. It wasn't working.

Then I saw Leah. "I thought you were going to ask a boy to dance if you didn't get asked," I said.

"I am." Leah sounded confident, exactly how I didn't feel. "I'm giving it ten more minutes. If no one asks me by then, I'll do the asking."

We spent the next ten minutes checking out all the boys and deciding who we'd definitely ask, who was a maybe, and who we'd NO WAY EVER ask.

CATEGORIES OF BOYS

YES, DEFINITELY!

↑ cute guy

charming, ↑ sure-of-
himself-without-being-
vain guy

↑ handsome AND nice guy

MAYBE, NOT SURE...

↑ shy, you-really-can't-tell guy

↑ smart and sweet, but maybe there's-an-edge guy

↑ funny, warm, friendly guy— those things go a long way even if a guy isn't really cute

The ten minutes were up, and we'd just finished sorting all the boys into categories when Kip, who was in the Maybe group, came up and asked Leah to dance. She shrugged, then smiled, then waved good-bye to me. I was all alone again. I looked for Carly and she was dancing with another boy. I saw Maxine dancing with some guy from the Yes, Definitely category. There were lots of kids dancing, but I wasn't one of them. I stood there, trying to look like I was doing exactly what I wanted to be doing — as if watching other people have fun was how I'd planned to spend my time.

I kept trying to catch Carly's eye. She'd come to the dance with me like she'd promised, but she'd abandoned me once we were there. What kind of friend does that?

The kind having fun! I stood there, getting madder and madder. By the time Carly FINALLY walked over to me, I was so furious, steam was coming out of my nose and ears — at least it felt that way.

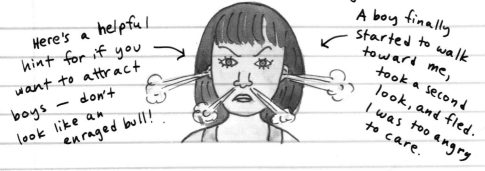

Here's a helpful hint for if you want to attract boys — don't look like an enraged bull!

A boy finally started to walk toward me, took a second look, and fled. I was too angry to care.

Carly was all laughing and sweaty and happy. I was fuming. It was a highly combustible combination.

"Hey," Carly said, "this is a great dance! Are you having fun?"

"Fun? FUN?!" I roared. "Yeah, it's a real thrill to stand here and watch everyone ELSE enjoy themselves! How could you leave me here ALL BY MYSELF LIKE A LOSER!"

"I came to the dance to <u>dance</u>," Carly sad flatly. "So sooooorry if that's what I'm doing. It's not <u>my</u> fault you're not dancing too."

I hate arguing with Carly because she's always at least partly right, even if she isn't completely right. I knew it wasn't her fault that nobody had asked me to dance, but I was too furious to back down.

"Go dance, then!" I yelled. "I'm leaving!"

"You do that," Carly said, as cold as ice. "I'm here to dance, not babysit."

It was our worst fight ever. I know I've said this before, but _this_ fight really was.

I walked home in the cool night air and let myself cry. I wasn't sure which hurt most — no one asking me to dance or Carly thinking I'm a little kid now, not up to her level. No, that's not true. I knew which bothered me most — Carly. I can bear not being pretty, but I can't bear Carly pulling away from me because I'm not grown up enough for her. I can be mature without being pretty. I just have to prove that to Carly.

I couldn't help wondering if I'd worn makeup, would everything have been different? Was this all my fault? →

← Would I have looked prettier? Would boys have asked me to dance? Would Carly think better of me, like I was more mature, even if boys _didn't_ ask me?

When I got home, I didn't want to go in. I didn't want Cleo to smirk and gloat and say, "Nyaah, nyaah, told you so!" So I sat outside until I was too cold and __had__ to go in. I hoped it was late enough that I could pretend I'd had a great time and hadn't stomped off, leaving the dance early.

Mom was watching TV and eating popcorn. There was no sign of Cleo. It seemed so cozy and warm, I plopped down next to Mom and started watching too. I couldn't follow what was happening because it was already halfway over, but that didn't matter. I was happy just not thinking, not talking, not feeling.

At the commercial I asked Mom where Cleo was. She said she was out with friends. That means I wasted my time freezing by the front door. Oh, well.

Then Mom asked how the dance was. I shrugged and said it was okay.

"Did you dance?" Mom asked.

I shook my head. "Not really. I didn't want to." which wasn't a total lie — even if a boy had asked me, I'm not sure I _did_ want to dance, but I definitely didn't want to look like a loser and dance by myself.

"Oh, Amelia, nobody asked you?" Mom put her arm around me and hugged me. "I can't imagine why not. You're very pretty."

"In your unbiased opinion," I grumbled.

Mom smiled and kissed the top of my head. "Yes, in my completely objective view. Don't worry, the next dance will be easier."

I sat bolt upright. "Oh, no! There _is_ no next dance! I'm done! I'm not going to another dance EVER!"

"Isn't that a bit melodramatic?" Mom said, trying to soothe me. But now I didn't want to be comforted. I wanted to be angry — it was better than being sad.

I remember _my_ first dance...

It was too late. Mom was in nostalgia-land, which meant I had to listen to boring stories about boring dances from a million years ago when Mom was young.

Mom was no help. I wished I could talk to Carly. I needed to explain why I got mad. I needed her to apologize. I needed something, but I wasn't sure what. So I wrote to Nadia, my old best friend. When I first moved away, we wrote to each other all the time. Now we do it less, but I still feel like I can tell Nadia anything.

Dear Nadia,
 HELP! 7th grade just started and already it's AWFUL. We had the first dance, and I didn't want to go, but Carly made me, and it was a <u>disaster</u>! No one asked me to dance (I <u>knew</u> that would happen!), but the worst part was Carly promised to keep me company and then she abandoned me. I didn't mean she had to babysit me, but she had to be a <u>friend</u>, didn't she? We had a horrible fight over it. Maybe I'm just not ready for 7th grade.
P.S. Do you think I'm pretty?
yours till the tear drops,
 Amelia

Nadia Kurz
61 South St.
Barton, CA
 91010

I used to think I could mail my troubles away by sending them to Nadia. Now it's not so easy, but I still felt lighter after I finished the letter.

I spent the next day waiting for Carly to call and apologize. She didn't. And she didn't call on Sunday, either. Walking to school on Monday, I thought how quickly 7th grade was ruined. The school year had just started and already it was horrible.

My first class was science, fortunately one without Carly, but she might as well have been there because suddenly all I could see was how many girls wore makeup. Out of 13 girls, 9 wore makeup — 10 if I counted the teacher, Ms. Trotsky. I was beginning to feel like a freak, a naked-faced freak.

Some girls wore a <u>lot</u> of makeup.

I like Ms. Trotsky. She's a good teacher. Even if she wears makeup.

Some girls wore a little.

But it looked like only nerds and the totally unpopular girls wore none. What did that make me?

I wondered if Carly was right after all to be mad at me. If she stayed my friend, would she ruin her reputation as a cool kid? It was one thing to be my friend in 6th grade — things were different in 7th.

I decided that when I saw her in English, I'd apologize. I wanted to be a good friend, with or without makeup.

Carly was already in class, reading, when I walked in. I noticed she was still wearing eyeliner. I guess now that she's started, she's keeping that look.

I sat down next to her and whispered, "Hey, I'm sorry about the dance. I was an idiot." She looked at me and said, "yes, you were."

"Hey," I said. "I apologized! Can't you accept that nicely?"

"Okay." She rolled her eyes. "But you were really awful, such a big baby!"

"I said I was sorry." I sighed. "Are we still friends?"

"Of course we are," Carly said, but she didn't sound very convincing.

Then Ms. Hanover started teaching and we couldn't talk anymore, but it wasn't a friendly silence.

By the time the bell rang for lunch, it felt like a wall of ice had frozen between us. There was so much cold air, I wasn't sure if we were going to eat together, even though we always did. I had to do something, so I tried to chip away at Carly's frostiness.

"Carly, can we talk about this?" I kept my voice soft and friendly.

"Sure." She shrugged. She didn't look at me.

"Hey, I was upset because you were like a different person at the dance, a flirty girl wearing makeup. I didn't recognize you! And you're still different now. Are you going to wear eyeliner all the time now? Is that the kind of person you want to be? I thought you said makeup was a waste of time and money, and you're naturally beautiful. I thought you didn't want to be like Cleo."

I don't want to be like Cleo and I am naturally beautiful. But I'm also growing up. To me, that means wearing some makeup — like my mom, like most women. I'm not overdoing it. I'm not a clown. I'm not Cleo— that's your fear about makeup, not mine. I'm in 7th grade now. I can't stay a little girl just so you're more comfortable with me. Being a friend means accepting someone the way they are, not trying to change them.

"I do accept you," I said. "I just wish we had talked about this whole makeup thing first. I understand why you want to wear it, and you look nice — you really do. But I'm not sure I'm ready for it myself. I know you're growing up — we both are — but can't it be more gradual? Can't we slow things down? I'm not in a hurry to start looking like a woman. I don't think I can, even if I wanted to. Can you accept me being slower than you? Can you still be my friend if I don't wear makeup or go to dances?"

There was a loooooong silence, painfully long. Finally Carly said, "I'll think about it."

I was furious! I was supposed to accept her, but she didn't have to accept me? I chewed my sandwich ferociously to keep myself from yelling at her. I didn't want to shout something I'd regret later. What I wanted to say was, does growing up mean turning on your friend? How mature is that? But I was afraid she would say she wasn't just growing up, she was outgrowing me. And I wondered, had she?

I remember that in preschool, I was best friends with a girl named Susie. We did everything together. Then somehow once we started kindergarten, I couldn't stand her. She was boring and annoying. That's when Nadia became my best friend. Was Carly outgrowing me the way I'd outgrown Susie?

The rest of the day, we were polite to each other, but not exactly friendly. My last class was art and Carly's was science, but we agreed to walk home together. That was something, at least.

In art, I saw that Leah was wearing makeup now too. Who would've guessed that a dance would create such big shifts in people?

Leah came up to me, all excited and happy.

Wasn't that a great dance on Friday? I had so much fun! And I think Kip really likes me. He's sooooo cute! I don't think he's a maybe guy anymore. He's a yes, Definitely!

What happened to you? Did you leave early?

That was a subject I didn't feel like talking about, so I talked about art class instead.

Have you decided what you're going to do for your self-portrait yet? I have no ideas. I'm not sure how I see myself.

It was true. I don't know if I'm pretty, if I want to wear makeup, if I want to grow up. What does that say about me as a person? Am I my face, my face changed with makeup, or what's inside? Who am I?

"I know what I'm going to do," Leah said. "I'm drawing myself as a superhero because that's who I <u>want</u> to be."

Fastest pen, surest pencil, most agile brush, able to draw or paint anything or anybody — it's Super Artist   LEAH!

I love Leah's idea. I wish I'd thought of it first. I'm more confused than ever.

Maybe that's what I'll make — a big question mark.
→

I'm not sure who I really am or who I want to be.
↙

I may not be sure who I am, but I <u>do</u> know who Carly is, and no matter what, I don't want to lose her as a friend. I tried to think of that as we walked home.

"Carly," I said. "We've had fights before and we've argued about LOTS of things, but in the end we always appreciate each other. That's what makes us such good friends. Now that we're in 7th grade, do I have to wear makeup for you to like me? Is that what you're saying, after all we've been through?"

"Of course not!" Carly said. "And I've never judged you by your looks."

"Ouch!" I winced. "Am I that ugly?"

"No, of course not. I didn't mean that. But you remember last year, how Maxine made fun of your hair, your clothes, your shoes..."

"How could I forget?" I was feeling beyond makeup now. If I had to draw a self-portrait that minute, it'd be a shadow on the ground, something trying desperately to disappear.

"Well, I saw you clearly then and I see you clearly now," Carly said. "I like you, Amelia, I really do. I'm just trying to figure out who I want to be, how I want to grow up."

She still liked me! That was all that mattered.

"I'm doing those things too," I said. "Can we do them together

Carly stopped walking and stared up at the deep blue sky. Then she looked at me and smiled.

"We can try."

I was so happy, I wanted to do a cartwheel. Instead I grabbed Carly's hand and shook it.

"It's a deal. We'll both try."

We ended up going over to Carly's house and doing our homework together. I've always liked Carly's mom — she's a nice, straightforward person, and she's genuinely interested in other people and what they think. I like that she talks to me as if I'm a grown-up, not a little kid. But today, I looked at her more closely.

I knew Ms. Tremain wore makeup, but I never noticed how elegant she looks.

My mom's a total slob compared to her. Even her fingernails are beautifully manicured. My mom chews her nails.

No wonder Carly wants to wear make up. She sees how good her mom looks — and she has a mom who can help her with her own make up. I don't have that kind of example. Instead, I have Cleo. I told my theory to Carly.

I think one reason I'm not sure about make up is my mom doesn't wear any. The only person in my house who does is Cleo - yuck! If I had your mom . . .

Go ahead and borrow her! I'm sure my mom would be happy to show you how to put on make up. Wanna try? If you don't like it, you can wash it off.

So we asked Ms. Tremain and she said yes, of course. She sat me down and very lightly, very gently, she showed me how to use eyeshadow and eyeliner and lipstick. And the way she did it, I actually looked pretty. I was amazed.

Wow! I can be pretty!

I look so different.'

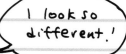

So grown-up!

"Not so different," Carly said. "You're pretty <u>without</u> makeup too, you know. That stuff can help, but it can't totally change your face."

Just then Carly's older brother, Marcus, walked in. He took one look at me and started to gag — I mean it, literally.

"What did you DO to her?" he choked. "You're ruining Amelia! You're turning her into a Pod Person!"

"Don't be ridiculous." Carly rolled her eyes. "Amelia looks great, and you   just don't like makeup."

You're right — I DON'T! And my opinion should count more than yours. Don't girls wear this junk to attract boys?

Well, I'm telling you — as a professional male — that the artificial look is NOT appealing for a lot of us. I want to see a girl for REAL, not a fake.

↑
Marcus is one of the hottest — and coolest — boys I know. Plus he's in high school, which automatically makes his opinion VERY valuable.

I didn't know who or what to believe. I wanted to ask Marcus if he thought I was pretty without makeup, but I didn't dare.

Marcus shrugged. "Okay, don't believe me. Just ask yourself, who is all this gunk really for — yourself or a guy?" He started to stomp off, then turned and said, "And ask yourself what kind of guy you WANT to attract — the kind who likes you for who you are or the kind who likes a mask?"

Carly glared at his back. "Don't listen to him!"

Ms. Tremain smiled. "He has a point. Those are good questions. Some women wear makeup to please themselves — I do. Not that your father complains about it. He likes it too. But, Amelia, honey, this is your choice. There's no one right way to look. Either way, you're beautiful."

I studied my face in the mirror. I looked good, I really did, but I couldn't help it — it didn't feel like me. I couldn't stop thinking about what Marcus said. What if some guy liked the fake me and had no idea who I really was? What if he saw me without makeup one day?

I wanted to be pretty on my own, not because of makeup. So I washed it all off. The funny thing was, I liked my face better without it. I could finally see myself.

And I think Carly saw me more clearly too.

"I'm glad you at least tried makeup," she said. "I felt like you were judging me, thinking I was vain or shallow because of a little eyeliner."

"I would never think that!" I shook my head. It was the total opposite of what I really thought — that she was too cool for me, too mature. "Maybe next time we should tell each other what we feel instead of imagining the other person's opinion. We were both completely wrong." I told Carly my fears about her outgrowing me.

She smiled. "You're right. We were both totally off base. We had a huge fight over nothing!"

When I got back home, Mom was already there, cooking dinner. I looked at her, really looked at her. I had to admit Carly's mom looked __much__ prettier. My mom's kind of frumpy, to be honest. If I had a choice of looking like her or like Ms. Tremain, I'd definitely choose Ms. Tremain.

Even makeup and better clothes might not help Mom. She has no style. She's just not that kind of woman.

"What are you staring at?" she asked, stirring a pot of sauce.

"I'm wondering why you don't wear makeup," I blurted out.

Mom snorted. "Why bother? Who am I trying to impress?"

"No one," I said. "Yourself. You could wear it to feel good about yourself, like Carly's mom does."

"I feel fine about myself." Mom shook her head. "I'd have pretty shaky self-esteem if lipstick and rouge could make a difference that way."

Mom isn't pretty, but she isn't ugly, either. She's someone who doesn't care about looks. →

← She's not the kind of woman I want to be, but I'm not sure yet WHO I want to become — just an older me, I guess.

Just then Cleo came home. She was a living advertisement warning against the perils of too much makeup.

You guys talking about LIPSTICK? About ROUGE?

You two? The naked faces in the house?

"Yeah," I lied. "We were talking about you, how fake you look."

Cleo batted her eyelashes. "What's wrong with fake? Fake is good. Fake is beautiful. Let me guess — you're still sad about the dance and now you're thinking that if you'd had on some face magic, someone would've asked you to dance."

"NO!" I said. "That's NOT what I'm thinking."

"Tell you what," Cleo offered, "for the next dance you can use my makeup. I'll even help you put it on so you don't mess it up."

"No, thanks! If I look like you, I'll really scare off guys!"

"You're just jealous," Cleo sniffed. "I'm sorry I was so nice to you."

"Girls, stop it!" Mom growled. "That's enough. You can use makeup or not, but you can't tease each other about the personal choices you make. After all, you might change your minds later. Amelia, you might decide to wear a little makeup, and Cleo, you might stop using it — or at least use <u>less</u>."

I shrugged. Maybe that was true, but Cleo was annoying with or without a fake face. Some things you can't disguise, no matter how hard you try.

After dinner that night, I wrote a story.

Facing the Truth

There was once a girl whose face was absolutely blank. You would think this would make things easy for her — she could be whoever she wanted to be. She could look any way she imagined.

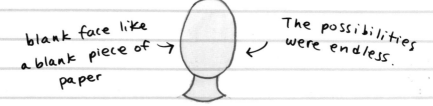

blank face like a blank piece of paper →

← The possibilities were endless.

Every morning she would choose her eyes, nose, mouth, and eyebrows.

Some days she was perky and cheerful.

Other days she was mysterious and elegant.

And others she was strong and fierce.

But after years of many different faces, the girl felt very confused. "Who am I _really_," she wondered. "I want one face that can fit all my moods."

"I want," she said, "a face that is truly ME."

Her mother explained that she could choose one face, but there was no going back, no changing her mind. She had better be certain she picked the face that was really her. Otherwise she would live the rest of her life with the wrong face.

And her mother began to cry. Tears poured down her face.

"What's wrong?" asked the faceless girl. "Why are you crying?"

"Because," her mother sobbed, "when I was your age, I wanted to have only one face too. I tried them all on, and there was one that felt right, like it was really me, but there was another one that I liked more, because it was prettier. So I chose the prettier face, thinking I was lucky to have the choice, but as soon as I put it on, I knew it was WRONG. It wasn't me at all! But it was too late — I was stuck with the wrong face, with looking like someone who wasn't me." The mother looked hard at the girl's blank face. "Don't make the same mista

The girl had always thought that her mother was very beautiful, but now she saw how sad she was — beautiful but sad. And now she understood why her mother had always seemed to hold a secret sorrow. The girl had imagined a broken heart, a lost love, not a false face.

The girl decided to be very careful with her choice. "I hope the real me isn't ugly — and that I'll recognize my real face when I find it," she said. She wondered if she'd have the courage to put on a hideous face even if she was sure it was the right one.

She searched through hundreds of faces. Many were cute or pretty. Some were beautiful. None felt right.

Finally, at the very bottom of the pile, when the girl was about to give up and accept being blank for the rest of her life, she saw it — her face! After all her doubts, she knew it right away. The eyes were friendly, the mouth turned up in a smile, and the nose fit perfectly in between. She couldn't say whether it was a pretty face or not. She just knew it was hers.

She put it on and immediately she felt whole, complete.
"This is me!" she yelled.

And even though it turned out her new eyes
needed glasses and her new teeth needed braces,
the girl knew she'd made the right choice.
Because she'd chosen herself.

The End

Okay, it's not a great story, but it's how I feel. I
like my face as it is because it's mine, it's _me_, and I'm
not ready to change it yet with makeup. To me, wearing
makeup is like saying I'm not good enough without it. I
know that's not how Carly and Leah feel, but it's how I
feel. At least for now. I reserve the right to change
my mind — maybe in 8th grade.

I brought my notebook to school and showed Carly my story because I thought it would help her understand me better, but that's not exactly what happened.

"It's a good story," Carly said. "I get it, really I do. But I'm not any less honest than you are. I'm not less true to myself because I'm wearing eyeliner."

"I know you're not. I didn't say you were." But I have to admit that I really do think that. I feel like Carly's a weaker person than before, that she's given in to all the media messages that say girls should look a certain way. Next thing you know, she'll have an eating disorder and get really skinny.

I have to admit, I respect Carly less because she's wearing makeup the way girls are told they should. I have to admit it to myself, but I'd NEVER tell Carly that.

On TV girls all look the same — very thin, usually blonde, with their stomachs showing in tight, tight tops. I know I don't look like that — and I don't want to! I'd make a terrible blonde!

↓

Sometimes I think they're all clones of the same person, they seem so interchangeable.

↙

Luckily, before we could get into another fight, Social studies class started, and the Egg gave us a great assignment.

I like the Egg because he's so young and enthusiastic. He actually went to this middle school not that long ago!

For the first report of the year, the topic is Hidden History. There are a lot of interesting and important people who haven't received much historical attention because at the time they lived, they weren't noticed.

The achievements of women have largely been ignored through much of American history, but that doesn't mean there weren't women who made significant contributions to our culture and society. Your assignment is to "discover" one of these women and write a report describing why you think this person should be better known to all of us. It doesn't have to be an "unknown" woman, just an underappreciated one.

Carly and I looked at each other — what a great topic! It sounded like a report that would be fun to do. The big question was, if these women are "hidden," how do we find them?

A lot of kids had that same question. The Egg explained that the women could be in books, but instead of a page, maybe there's only a sentence or short paragraph mentioning them. Or they might be left out of our text-book entirely, but are in books that aren't known to most people. He suggested using the Internet to search for broad topics like "American Women World War II Pilots" or "American Women Scientists."

I love this idea! I don't know who I'll discover, but I'm sure of one thing — I'm picking a woman who didn't wear make up. I need a good model for that, someone other than my mom.

Anyway, the Egg said NO movie stars or fashion models because those people aren't hidden — they're famous.

And being in movies, being beautiful, isn't the kind of achievement he wants us to write about.

The assignment was good in another way — it gave Carly and me something to talk about besides make up (which we're stuck on lately).

At lunch we went to the library to start our search. Who did we run into? Maxine. I wished she was hidden!

Maxine is the terrible, nasty girl who tried to convince Carly I wasn't worth having as a friend last year. Then she turned on Carly, too. She was as trendy and stylish as ever — with lots of makeup. She completely ignored me, which was fine with me since I was ignoring her.

"See," I whispered to Carly, "you don't want to be like Maxine, the kind of person who's desperate to make an impression."

Carly frowned. "I'm nothing like Maxine. Why would you say that?"

"I didn't mean your personality is like hers." I realized too late that I was starting a fight, one I really didn't want to have.

"Then what did you mean? What exactly about me has ANY similarity to Maxine?" Carly's tone was frosty.

"Um, nothing. I was just talking," I mumbled, miserable.

"Nothing?" Carly raised an eyebrow. "I don't think so. Come on, Amelia, out with it. Say it!"

There was no way to avoid it. I couldn't change the subject. I couldn't come up with some bland generality to distract her. I couldn't pretend I hadn't heard her.

I looked down and quickly said, "Because you both wear makeup, but obviously you're much more discreet and tasteful than Maxine, who completely overdoes it."

Carly slammed shut the book she'd been leafing through.

"That does it!" she hissed. "I'm going. You can talk to me when you're ready to admit you're being unfair and judgmental — you're imposing your own choice on everyone else."

She left in a noisy huff. I felt awful because she was right.

Maxine glared at me, all alone now in the library, and she smiled an evil, gloating smile. I turned my back to her and tried to focus on finding amazing women. But all I could think of was Carly — she was amazing, and I wasn't being fair to her at all. I was judging her by her looks when she was so much more than that.

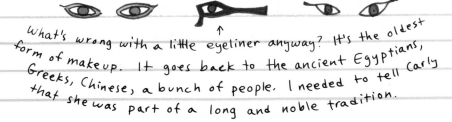

What's wrong with a little eyeliner anyway? It's the oldest form of makeup. It goes back to the ancient Egyptians, Greeks, Chinese, a bunch of people. I needed to tell Carly that she was part of a long and noble tradition.

I had been doing exactly what I didn't want Carly to do — judging someone by their looks. Only instead of coming down on someone for being ugly, I was criticizing Carly for being pretty, for caring about her looks.

That was really messed up. Suddenly a thought jolted through me — was I jealous? Was that why I was so hard on Carly? She was beautiful without makeup _and_ she knew how to use it to make herself even prettier. I wasn't beautiful to begin with, and when I wore makeup, I ended up looking like a clown. Or fake. I just couldn't pull it off.

Except when Carly's mom helped me with makeup. Then I looked good — even pretty. →

I just didn't feel like myself. But maybe I could get used to looking like that. Maybe I should give being pretty a chance. Maybe Marcus is wrong about what boys like.

I was more confused than ever, but one thing was clear — whether _I_ wore makeup or not, I had to accept Carly wearing it. I had to be nice about it. I had to apologize. And I _can't_ be jealous of my best friend.

Carly avoided me for the rest of the day, so I couldn't tell her how sorry I was. I tried calling her once I got home, but there was no answer. I left a lame message and sent an even lamer e-mail.

I admit I made a mistake with Carly, but why do girls get stuck with these kinds of hard choices — makeup or not?

What does the choice say about you? How do you choose? Boys are lucky. They don't have to think about the complicated things girls do. They have much more basic choices.

Carly avoided me the next day and the day after that. I tried passing her notes, but she wouldn't take them. I left one in her locker and she put it back in mine. I didn't know what to do.

Instead of eating lunch with Carly, I sat with Leah and we talked about our self-portrait ideas. I like Leah, but I really missed Carly. I had to think of some way to show her how sorry I was.

But I also had to find a subject for my Hidden (or Forgotten) Woman report. Since the fight with Carly, I hadn't done any work on it. So I made myself go back to the library. Carly wasn't there (too bad), but neither was Maxine (phew!).

I stared at the computer for a while, thinking of the amazing friend I'd lost. Then I got to work — it was time to find someone. And I did — I discovered some truly incredible women I'd never heard of before. At first I thought I'd write about Harriet Quimby, the first woman to fly an airplane across the English Channel.

← She sounded like someone w was perfect for Carly becaus she was a newspaper reporte like Carly wants to be — as wel as an aviator.

I thought Carly might pick her, so I looked for another subject, and I found Jackie Mitchell. She was a young woman who pitched on a regular men's baseball team. She was really good, and the first team she pitched against was the New York Yankees.

She struck out Babe Ruth, Lou Gehrig, and Tony Lazzeri — for real! No one believed a woman could play baseball like that, but Jackie Mitchell proved them wrong.

It was a great story, but I'm not into baseball. I wanted to write about a woman who could really be a model for me.

Then I found the perfect person, Georgia O'Keefe. She was a brilliant artist, and her paintings were strong and bold, not frilly and pretty, the way people expected a woman to paint. She lived to be very old, and her art just got better the older she grew. That was a real model for me. Best of all, I loved the photo of her I found. She looked wise and strong and very beautiful, even though her face was etched with wrinkles and she wore no makeup at all.

There was something deeply honest about her, like she knew herself well.

I wanted to be like her. I tried to draw her, but I couldn't get close to how she held herself.

I was so caught up in my research, I didn't notice that Carly had come into the library until she sat down next to me. I jumped at the chance to apologize.

Carly, I'm REALLY sorry. I know I was wrong, totally wrong. I've thought about it a lot, believe me.

I know. I believe you. And it's okay. I'm not mad anymore.

"You're not?" I was surprised.

"No," said Carly. "In some ways you're right. Wearing makeup isn't as simple as I want it to be. I don't want to be influenced by the media and how it says girls should look, but I admit I am. I'm trying to be more conscious of it, but those messages are EVERYWHERE. I wish I could be as free of them as you are. I admire that in you, Amelia."

"You do?" I could feel my cheeks turn red. "I really admire you. I was just thinking that you're like one of these amazing hidden women I'm learning about."

Carly grinned. "Except, of course, I haven't done anything important."

"Yet," I added. "I'm sure you will."

I told her about the women I'd found and how I'd chosen Georgia O'Keefe for my topic. She agreed that she's a good subject. She liked Harriet Quimby, but she's already started her report. She's writing about Phillis Wheatley, a woman who was born in Africa, sold as a slave in America when it was still a British colony, and went on to become a famous poet.

In her lifetime, she was famous. Now she's completely forgotten. I was surprised I'd never heard of her before when once she was so well-known. She's exactly the kind of person the Egg wanted us to discover.

Carly showed me a drawing of what she looked like. →

Even though she had three things going against her — being a woman, an African, and a slave — she learned how to read and write. She was so good, she had her poetry published!

"I just wish she'd been more political." Carly sighed. "She never spoke out against slavery. Instead, she wrote a poem saying it was a blessing to be taken from Africa because she became a Christian. She conveniently didn't mention becoming a slave."

I smiled. No wonder we're so critical of our friends when even our heroes can't measure up. I guess we all have things people can pick at.

"Yeah, I bet she even wore makeup," I teased.

Carly laughed. "Okay, I'm being too hard on her. She accomplished a lot. She did what was important to her — I can't expect her to do what _I_ would have done."

And just like that, we were best friends again. Just in time, too, because there's <u>another</u> dance coming up. At lunch the next day that's all anyone talked about.

Carly ↓

Leah ↓

Me ↓

"Come on, Amelia," Carly insisted. "Give it another chance."

"Yeah. Try wearing makeup this time," Leah said.

"Why go?" I said. "No one's going to ask me to dance this time either. Why make myself miserable?"

Carly looked at me. "Would Georgia O'Keefe give up? Would Phillis Wheatley? What about Harriet Quimby or Jackie Mitchell? Show some courage!"

I rolled my eyes. "It's a dance, Carly, not a major achievement."

"My point exactly!" Carly grinned.

I can't believe it, but I gave in. I said I'd go, which means another disaster. If I don't already have a bad reputation from the last dance, I will after this one.

Luckily, when I got home, there was a card from Nadia. That cheered me up!

Dear Amelia,

I so wish I could help you becuz I know just how you feel. Our first dance was last week. Don't ask me why I went – sheer stupidity, I guess – but I did and spent the whole time by the snack table. My friend Roxanne told me that I should have worn makeup, but I hate that idea. Am I wrong? Should I wear makeup?

Yours till the lip sticks, Nadia

Expanding Horizons

80¢

Amelia
564 N. Homerest
Oopa, Oregon
97881

(P.S. Yea - you are pretty.)

Amazing! Nadia's having the exact same problems as me. No wonder we're still such good friends. It felt better knowing I wasn't the only one worrying about makeup. I had no idea what to tell her.

I tried to write her back.
↓

Dear Nadia,
   I know JUST how you feel.
I can't figure out the whole
makeup question either. All
my friends use it and I feel
like I should too, but I can't.
It feels fake to me, like lying.
Plus Marcus, a really cool guy,
told me that some boys — the
best ones, like him — <u>don't</u>
like makeup. I don't know
what to believe!
        yours till the face powders,
                        amelia

Nadia Kurz
61 South St.
Barton, CA
    91010

        But when I read my card over, I realized I hadn't
said anything useful. I tore it up and tried again and
again. Until I had a big pile of crumpled-up cards.
     So I gave up. I'll write to Nadia when I've figure
something out myself. I hope that's BEFORE 8th
grade!
     I wasted so much time on Nadia's non-letter, I
forgot that my self-portrait is due tomorrow. I had
to get to work! The problem was, I still had no
idea what to do. I mean, who am I, anyway?

And I'm so confused about my face right now. Am I pretty or not? Does my face really represent _me_ or is it just how I happen to look? What does my face say about me?

I wasn't getting anywhere when I noticed my Georgia O'Keefe report. (At least I finished _that_.) I love the photos her husband took of her — she had an expressive face, so sure of exactly who she was. I wanted a self-portrait like that. I wanted to be confident, not confused. I wanted my face and my personality to match perfectly, the way hers did.

She paints sort of like this.
O'Keefe's paintings have bright colors and bold shapes, and you can feel the crisp air in her pictures. →

I'm not that kind of an artist, not that kind of strong personality. I need words as much as pictures, which is why I have so many notebooks.

NOTEBOOKS! _That's_ who I am! I'm what I pour into my notebooks!

I felt like I was having one of those → flashing cartoon ideas.

Suddenly I knew just ← what to do and how to do it!

First I made a black silhouette of my profile like I remember making in 5th grade.

↓

Then I glued a small notebook on top.

Inside the pages, I glued in stuff cut out of my old notebooks — nothing too private, since other kids will see this.

The self-portrait turned out great — I really felt like it represented me. I may not know yet who I'll grow up to be, but I do know who I am right now. I was so proud of how it turned out, I showed the self-portrait to Mom. I could tell she was impressed.

This is beautiful, Amelia! What an interesting idea!

Even Cleo couldn't insult it, though she tried. →

yeah, not bad — for a 7th grader.

"What about the dance that's coming up?" Cleo asked. "Are you going? Maybe this time you'll take my advice and wear something decent."

"I don't need your advice," I said. "I'm borrowing something from Carly again — she has real style." I wish I could borrow other things from Carly too, like how easy it is for her to be in crowds, how nothing makes her nervous, how everyone likes her. Too bad that's not possible. I'm already anxious.

I made a chart to measure what it takes to make someone nervous. Carly's at the top of non-nervousness. I'm practically at the bottom, where EVERYTHING worries you.

It's funny — some things don't make me nervous at all – like having the whole class see my self-portrait. But going to a dance is something else entirely.

The next day, I ran into Carly before art class, so I showed her my project.

"It's great," she said. "See, that's one of the things I like about you — you're so creative."

I couldn't stop smiling.

Then the bell rang. Carly grabbed my hand. "And you'll be fine at the dance, I know you will!" She squeezed my fingers, then rushed off to class.

It was ~~weird~~ ~~wierd~~ ~~weird~~ ~~wierd~~ ~~weird~~ ~~wierd~~ weird — just that pressure on my hand made me feel more ↑ confident. Or maybe it was because I was proud HELP! of my self-portrait. Either way, suddenly I wasn't as worried about the dance tonight. I had gone from a six to an eight on the Nerve-O-Meter.

Even in 7th grade, I can't get this word right!

I tried to picture myself dancing with a boy. It didn't make me nervous to imagine it, but it seemed ← like total fantasy, like something that would NEVER actually happen.

Leah loved my self-portrait and so did Ms. Oates.
I was really impressed by what the other kids had
done. One especially made me laugh because it was
exactly the kind of thing I've been thinking
about lately.

This girl Jackie had cut
parts of faces from magazines
and made a collage poking fun
at the stereotypes of what's
beautiful, using advertising
slogans. At the very bottom
she'd glued on a kindergarten
picture of herself and labeled
it "The Real Me." The whole
thing was brilliant.

Who They Want Me to Be

Sparkle!
long, luscious lashes
Smooth skin
Shinier, Bouncier Hair

BOLD, WET COLOR
lips that pucker up
SMILE!

No more freckles!

Cleaner, Whiter Teeth

The Real Me

I had to tell her how much
I liked it.

I love your piece!
I've been thinking the same
things.

Thanks. It's
ridiculous that there's so
much pressure to look a
certain way. And if it's this
strong for us now, what will
it be like in college?

The strange thing is, Jackie is so beautiful,
she doesn't need to pay attention to advertisements
at all. She's naturally gorgeous.

Some of the portraits by boys were fascinating —
like glimpses into an alien creature's mind.

One boy took a
rock and drew
a bland face
on it with a
marker.

Another boy glued
all these little green
plastic army men
together into one
big, hulking soldier.

Sam took a paper
bag, cut out eye-
holes, and glued
photos of his actual
eyes behind the holes
so it looked like a
real person was
under the bag.

The whole class got into a
great discussion about how we
see ourselves compared to how other people view
us. It was really interesting. Maybe art will help
me figure out who I really am, the way it did for
Georgia O'Keefe, the way poetry did for Phillis
Wheatley.

"You know," Leah said as we left class together,
"you could look at wearing makeup as a kind of art,
only instead of drawing on paper, you draw on your face.
Does thinking of it that way make you want to be
artistic on your face and wear makeup to the dance?"

I smiled. "I like looking at it that way, but I think for now I like my face the way it is. We're only in 7th grade — there's plenty of time for makeup later."

"Like in 8th grade?"

I shrugged. "I was thinking maybe high school, but who knows?"

Carly was waiting for me so we could walk home together and get ready for the dance. When the dance started, I'd be on my own, but until then I had Carly with me. That helped.

Cleo was her usual obnoxious self that night.

Poor Amelia! Another dance, another failure. Why punish yourself?

Do you like standing in a corner by yourself?

"That's _not_ how I plan to spend the evening!" I snapped.

"Leave her alone!" Carly said.

"I will," huffed Cleo, "and so will everyone else. Too bad I won't see you when you slink back home. I've got a _date_ — byeeeee!"

She was gone, but her words stayed behind. I tried not to let them get to me, but it was hard. All my confidence had leaked out.

I felt bland and boring.

Cleo was right. →

why would anyone ask me to dance?

Carly tried to cheer me up. She helped me put together a cute outfit from the clothes she'd brought over.

"Are you sure you don't want a little makeup?" Carly asked. I shook my head. I just couldn't.

"Then how about nail polish?" she offered.

I smiled. Now that I could do. So Carly painted all my nails — fingers and toes — pale purple. I loved how it looked. It was like I was tiptoeing into makeup, not diving in completely.

← It's funny how such a small thing could make me feel pretty.

It was already crowded when we got to the dance. Aldo was waiting for Carly. Leah was dancing with Kip. I was by myself.

Jackie was also by herself, standing by the drinks table, so I went up to say hi.

Hey, Amelia. I didn't think you'd be here. You don't seem the type.

What type am I?

You know, the creative, artistic type.

So are you and you're here.

"Yes, well, I'm also the ever-optimistic type. You know, the tomorrow-will-be-a-better-day kind, the this-dance-will-be-fun-even-though-the-last-one-stank kind."

"That's me, too." I grinned. "And maybe this dance _will_ be better."

We stood there, listening to the music, thinking optimistic thoughts when the impossible happened. Two boys came up to us. One asked Jackie to dance, and the other asked me.

ME!!! ○ ○ ○

I was so happy to be asked, I didn't even look closely at the boy. Only once we were on the dance floor did I realize it was Zachary, the boy in my art class who'd made the rock face.

"Funny, you don't look like a rock now," I yelled over the music.

"Well, you don't look like a notebook," he yelled back. He was blushing!

He was as nervous as me! I'd just assumed it was easy for the boy — all he had to do was ask a girl to dance. He was in control, while us girls could only wait and hope some guy would pick us.

It reminded me of choosing teams for softball — how I ALWAYS got picked last. It was that same awful kind of waiting.

↓

But maybe it wasn't easy to ask, either. What if the girl said no? That would be terrible, like a slap in the face. I almost wanted to thank Zachary for being brave enough to ask me, but that would've been dorky, so I didn't.

Instead I blurted out something even worse. I said it before I knew I was saying it — it was awful!

"I hope you don't mind that I'm not wearing make up."

That's it. That's what I said. As soon as the words were out of my mouth, I wanted to be invisible.

Zachary just grinned. "That's what I like about you."

Now it was my turn to blush. "Really?" I squeaked.

He nodded. So Marcus was right — some guys don't like make up, just like some girls don't. The funny thing was, dancing like that, with Zachary looking at me, I felt beautiful.

Not that he's my boyfriend or anything like that.

It was just a dance, but it was great!

Then across the dance floor, I saw Carly and Aldo. Carly looked over and saw me at the same moment. There were lots of kids dancing around us and music filled the spaces in between. Carly and I looked at each other and grinned. We were both beautiful and we knew it. That was the best part of the dance for me.

I think 7th grade will be a really good year for me after all — and I finally have an answer for Nadia.